Word List

Here is a list of words that might make it easier
to read this book. You'll find them in boldface the
first time they appear in the story.

Invisible	in-VI-zuh-buhl
Champagne	sham-PAYN
caviar	KA-vee-ar
glamorous	GLAM-ruhs
limousines	LI-muh-zeenz
outrageous	out-RAY-juhs
production	pruh-DUHK-shun
character	KAIR-ik-ter
commissary	KO-muh-sair-ee
wardrobe	WOR-drohb
chandelier	shan-duh-LEAR
digital	DI-juh-tuhl
supervisor	SOO-per-veye-zer
technicians	tek-NI-shunz
tech	tek
klutz	kluhts
hurricane	HER-uh-kayn
flexible	FLEK-suh-buhl
techniques	tek-NEEKS

A Change of Direction

BARBIE and associated trademarks are owned by and used under license from Mattel, Inc. © 1999 Mattel, Inc. All Rights Reserved. Published by Grolier Books, a division of Grolier Enterprises, Inc. Story by Victoria Saxon. Photo crew: Paul Jordan, Laura Lynch, Susan Cracraft, Lars Auvinen, Jeremy Lloyd, Lisa Collins. Produced by Bumpy Slide Books. Printed in the United States of America.

ISBN: 0-7172-8887-0

GROLIER
B O O K S

When the three o'clock bell rang, Skipper felt too excited to walk home from school. She wanted to run. As soon as she turned the corner onto her block, she started jogging. When she got to her front yard, she couldn't wait any longer. She ran up the front walk and flung open the door.

"Barbie!" she shouted. "Are you home? I have great news!"

"In here!" Barbie called from the living room.

"You'll never believe what happened," Skipper explained, trying to catch her breath. "I got an *A* on my final project in computer class."

"That's terrific, Sis!" Barbie replied. "And I thought you were just excited because it was the last day of school for the year."

"That's true, too," Skipper admitted. "But that's not all. My drama teacher has selected three of his students to try out for a part in a movie. And guess what? He chose me as one of the three!"

"Congratulations!" Barbie said proudly. "You know, Skip, when you put your mind to something, you can do anything."

"I know, I know," Skipper groaned, rolling her eyes at her big sister. Then she added seriously, "There's only one problem. The movie is your new film, *The **Invisible** Woman*."

"That's great news!" Barbie cried. "So what's the problem?"

Skipper explained, "I don't want to get the part just because you are the director. Do you think it's fair for me to audition?"

"Sure," Barbie answered. "I'll just call Cindy,

our casting director. I'll tell her not to give you any special treatment. And I won't even come to your audition. That way, everyone will have the same chance. How does that sound?"

Skipper thought for a moment. Then she smiled brightly and said, "Great! **Champagne** and **caviar,** here I come!"

Barbie frowned at her younger sister. "Watch it, young lady. You're still only sixteen. Besides," she added with a grin, "you do realize that *caviar* is just a fancy name for fish eggs?"

Skipper wrinkled her nose and replied, "All those **glamorous** movie stars eat it, so it must be good." Then the teenager pulled Barbie to her feet and twirled her around the room.

Barbie laughed and shook her head. "I'm just glad you'll finally be able to see where I work," she said. "You've only been bugging me about it forever!" The two sisters laughed.

A few days later, Skipper woke up bright and

early. She had hardly slept all night because she was so excited. It was the day of her audition. She tried on half the clothes in her closet, searching for the perfect shirt. Finally she went back to the first one she had tried on. She left the others on her bed. Then she ran downstairs to breakfast.

Skipper chattered away to her younger sister Stacie as she poured milk over her cereal. "Just think, Stace, I'll have my hair and makeup done every day. Maybe I'll even get to meet Len LaRusso."

"Oooh!" Stacie joked, making fun of her starstruck sister. "Len may be a movie star, but he's not half as cool as Super Glider. He's the best!"

"What do you know about movie stars, anyway?" Skipper shot back.

"All right, that's enough!" Barbie broke in. "Skipper, don't get your hopes up about Lenny. I just happen to know that he's shooting on location in London."

Skipper frowned, then brightened. "But my other favorite star, Diane Burns, is in the movie. So maybe I'll get to meet her. She's so glamorous."

Barbie sighed. "Yes, Diane's in the movie," she said, shaking her head. "I just don't know where you get these ideas about acting, Skip. It's not all fancy parties and **limousines.** It's a lot of hard work," she warned.

"But that's not what *Teen Dream* magazine says," Skipper protested. "They show pictures of beautiful movie stars riding in limousines, wearing fabulous clothes, going to **outrageous** parties. That's what I want to do."

Barbie added, "Well, I think it would be a great experience for you to be cast in a small role. Then you might get an idea of what the movie business is really like."

After breakfast, Barbie drove Skipper to the studio lot. At the entrance, a security guard opened the gate and waved them on. "Have a nice day, Ms. Roberts," he called. Barbie waved back as she drove through.

Out the window, Skipper could see rows of plain-looking buildings. The huge, boxlike buildings had rounded roofs and no windows.

"What are those?" Skipper asked her sister.

Barbie replied, "Those are the soundstages where most TV and movie scenes are shot. They're not very exciting to look at, are they?"

"No," Skipper answered. "But they look big enough to park an airplane inside!"

Barbie laughed. "Sometimes we do!"

After parking the car, Barbie pointed to a green building. "The casting director's office is in that building right there. I've got a ten o'clock meeting with the **production** designers. I'll be in soundstage number fourteen, right over there."

"Okay, I see it," Skipper said, nodding her head. "I'll meet you there when I'm done."

"Good luck," Barbie told her. "Or, as they say in show business, 'Break a leg!'"

"Thanks," Skipper replied. The sun beat down on her back as she crossed the parking lot. Despite the heat, Skipper realized, her hands were cold and clammy. When she opened the door to the building, she was hit by a blast of cold, air-conditioned air. The receptionist asked her to sign her name on a list. Then she handed Skipper a few pages from the script and told her to have a seat.

Skipper looked around the small waiting room. There were twelve other girls waiting, too. They all had long, blond hair and blue eyes. They were all about Skipper's age and size. Skipper couldn't believe it. It felt like looking in a dozen mirrors. "I guess they know what they want this person to look like," she thought. "I just hope that wasn't the only reason my teacher picked me to audition."

Skipper found a seat and quickly read over her lines. After reading a few pages, she realized something: If she got this role, she would have to do a scene with Diane Burns, the movie star! Her heart started pounding. She tried to concentrate and took a deep breath. Then she reached for a pencil and went through her part, line by line.

Time passed slowly. One girl after another was called in. A few minutes later, each one would come out. Some looked confident, while others looked upset.

Skipper looked at her watch. Could it be that only twenty minutes had passed? Just when she thought she would never be called, a man wearing glasses opened the door. "Skipper Roberts?" he read from his clipboard.

It was Skipper's turn to audition!

Chapter Two

Skipper stood up and straightened her shirt. She wondered whether she should have worn a different one. "Too late now," she mumbled to herself.

"What's that?" asked the man with the clipboard.

Skipper's face turned bright red. "Oh, nothing," she replied shyly.

As she followed the man into the next room, Skipper realized that her legs were trembling. The man sat down behind a long table. Three other people with pencils and paper were there waiting.

"Skipper?" said a woman with glasses.

"Yup, that's me," Skipper answered nervously. She thought, "Boy, I sound dumb!"

The woman smiled. "I'm Cindy, the casting director." She motioned to the woman on her right. "Maria will act as the other **character** in this scene. She'll read the lines with you. You can start whenever you're ready."

"Thanks," Skipper said, taking a deep breath. She wiped her sweaty palms on her pants, then began to read. But as soon as she spoke her first line, she heard someone at the table scribble on a piece of paper.

Skipper almost stopped. Then she remembered what Barbie had told her in the car: "Try not to be too nervous. Just be yourself. You'll be great." So she tried to relax during the other woman's lines. Pretty soon, Skipper's own lines started to feel more natural. She felt as if she were having a real conversation with Maria. She was even

11

starting to have fun!

Just then a loud voice interrupted them. "Thank you. That will be all."

Skipper looked up, startled. Everyone was scribbling more notes on their papers. Skipper didn't know what else to do except smile. "Thank you," she said. Her audition was over.

Confused, Skipper left the room. She hadn't even had a chance to finish her scene. "I guess no one liked me," she thought.

Skipper left the building and walked over to soundstage fourteen. Barbie was finishing up.

"How about some lunch at the **commissary**?" Barbie suggested. "My treat."

Skipper sighed and replied, "Would you mind driving me home instead?"

"Sure, no problem," Barbie answered, looking concerned. They walked to the car and drove out the studio gate.

Skipper stared out the window in silence.

Finally Barbie said, "Are you going to tell me what happened? Or am I going to have to guess?"

Skipper turned to look at her sister. "I don't think I did very well at my audition."

"Why do you say that?" Barbie asked her.

"They didn't even let me finish the scene," Skipper burst out. "They must have hated me!"

"Oh, Skipper," Barbie said kindly, "casting directors always do that. They're very busy. They have to audition actors all day long. They don't need to see you act out the whole scene in order to know whether you're right for the part."

Barbie turned the car into the driveway and parked. "Skip, you have to remember that casting directors are looking to see if you fit a role. They are not judging who you are inside. How did *you* feel about your reading? Did you enjoy yourself?"

"I guess so," Skipper answered. "At first I was nervous, but then something happened. I can't explain it, but suddenly it felt very natural. I almost forgot I was at an audition. I was surprised when the casting director asked me to stop."

Barbie smiled. "Then you did fine."

"I just hope Cindy thinks so," Skipper stated. "I want so much to become an actor."

"Well," Barbie explained, "you're already beginning to see what it's like. Remember that for each role an actor gets, she may go on ten or twenty auditions. It's just part of the job. You read for a part, then you wait."

Skipper frowned and said, "I think I'll like the reading part better than the waiting part."

And for the next two days, Skipper found out how right she was. She was so jumpy, she couldn't sit still. With the school year over, she checked the answering machine six times a day for messages. But she heard nothing. Finally, on the third day, Skipper checked the machine again, and the light was blinking! The message was from Cindy. Skipper could hardly believe her ears: She'd gotten the role!

Chapter Three

The next day there was a knock at Skipper's front door.

"Special delivery!" said the man in uniform. He was carrying a package addressed to Skipper. She signed for it and thanked him. Then she closed the door and quickly ripped open the package. It was her very own script for *The Invisible Woman!*

Although she was only in a couple of scenes, Skipper read the entire script not once, but twice. She remembered what her drama teacher had told her: It's important to read the entire script to better understand your character's role.

The story was about a woman who secretly found a way to make herself invisible. She used her special power to help people in need. Skipper was reading through her lines when the telephone rang. It was Barbie.

"Hi, Skipper!" she began. "Did you get your script?"

"Yes, I did," Skipper replied. "I'm just starting to memorize my lines. I don't have that many, but it can't hurt to be prepared."

"That's the spirit!" Barbie cheered. "Oops, I have to go. I'm needed back on the set. I'll see you later tonight."

"Okay," Skipper answered. "Good-bye!" Then she hung up the phone and finished reading the script one more time.

That night, it took Skipper a long time to get to sleep. She was so excited! When she finally slept, she tossed and turned, lines buzzing through her head.

Skipper's first day as an actor began at four o'clock in the morning, when her alarm clock rang. The room was still pitch black. She groaned and hopped out of bed. After her shower,  Skipper again rummaged through her closet to find the right outfit. Barbie had told her not to worry about what to wear. The **wardrobe** mistress would be giving Skipper her own costume. "I have to look my best on the set," Skipper thought as she put on some lipstick anyway.

"Are you ready for your first day of work?" Barbie asked during their quick breakfast.

"You know I am!" Skipper replied. "I've been waiting my whole life for this day!"

"Then let's go," Barbie answered.

Barbie and Skipper soon arrived on the set. Skipper was amazed to find that inside this huge soundstage, the crew had built sets. But they all were different. One looked like a fancy hotel lobby. Another looked like a dirty waiting room in a city train station. Yet another looked like a teenager's bedroom. The amazing part was that they were all lined up in a row. And each room was missing a wall so that you could see inside.

Barbie saw her younger sister staring at the sets and explained, "Sometimes walls get in the way of the cameras. When we build the sets, we leave one wall out. That way it will be easier to film the scenes. Today we're going to start filming the final scene in the movie."

Skipper broke in excitedly, "You mean the one in the beautiful hotel?"

"Yes," Barbie said, nodding. She pointed to a huge crystal **chandelier** hanging from the ceiling of the hotel set. "We don't always shoot in the order of the story. We shoot all the scenes that take place in the same location first. That way we can tear down a set and make room for another one."

"I'm surprised," Skipper replied. "I just figured you would start shooting from the beginning."

Barbie grinned and said, "You would think so, huh? But that's not how it works. Actually, doing it this way helps to keep costs down."

Just then a short, dark-haired woman bumped into Skipper. She wore glasses, a sweatsuit, and a baseball cap. "Excuse me," she apologized politely. "Morning, Barbie," she added with a wave as she walked away.

"Good morning, Diane," Barbie called, waving back.

Skipper's jaw dropped when she realized what Barbie had said. "That's not . . ." she said.

"Diane Burns, the movie star?" Barbie finished for her. "Yes, that's her. Really glamorous, isn't she?" Barbie asked, smiling.

"Not at all!" Skipper blurted out. "She looks

just like anyone else. And she's so *short!* She's no taller than me! And I'm still growing."

Barbie laughed out loud. Then she looked at her watch and said, "I need to get to work, Skip. The dressing area is over there." Barbie pointed to a row of white doors. "Why don't you check in with the makeup and wardrobe departments? You'll be called when you're needed."

"Thanks, Barbie," Skipper replied. She headed over to wardrobe.

Skipper met with the wardrobe mistress. She asked Skipper's clothing sizes. Then she handed her a pair of worn-looking jeans, a scratchy wool sweater, and a long winter coat. She also gave her a hat and scarf. The scene was going to take place in Chicago during the wintertime.

"Just put on a T-shirt with your jeans until you actually film the scene," the wardrobe mistress told her. "It gets hot on the set. And if you go outside, you'll roast. It's supposed to hit one hundred degrees today. We don't want you passing out from the heat!"

Skipper smiled and thanked her. "Maybe the fancy clothes will come in my next movie," she thought. Then she headed over to makeup.

Skipper soon found herself sitting in a high chair surrounded by mirrors and bright lights. The makeup artist used a cold, wet sponge to apply a thick, heavy makeup called pancake. Then he lined Skipper's lips with a dark pink pencil and filled them in with a lighter pink lipstick. He applied a gray eyeliner, eye

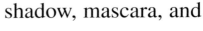

shadow, mascara, and

heavy blusher. Skipper had never had anyone else put makeup on her before. Her eyes kept watering. And she blinked every time the makeup artist came near them. She could tell that he was getting frustrated with her, but she couldn't help it. Finally he loaded a big powder puff with loose powder and applied it to her face and neck. "Try not to touch your face," the makeup artist told her.

When she was back in her dressing room, Skipper looked in the mirror. She hadn't had this much makeup on since she had dressed up as a clown for Halloween. "Nothing left to do but wait," she thought. So the young actor sat down with her script and began to review her lines.

Minutes passed. Hours passed. Skipper was expecting to be called at any time. But no one came. She was beginning to wonder if they had forgotten about her. She was getting very sleepy.

Suddenly there was a knock on her door. Skipper was so startled that she dropped her script. She hurried to answer the door. It was a young man with dark brown hair. He wore a plaid shirt and blue jeans. He introduced himself as Glenn, one of the production assistants. "You shouldn't have to wait much longer," he told her. "The director likes to take her time when she's shooting. Sometimes Ms. Roberts films scenes several times before they're right."

"Is it okay if I go outside and watch?" Skipper asked.

"Sure!" Glenn replied. "Just be careful not to make any noise while they're filming."

Skipper agreed and followed Glenn outside the soundstage to an outdoor set. It looked just like a city street lined with tall buildings. But when Skipper walked up to the set, she could see that the buildings were fake. They were nothing more than propped-up boards painted to look like city buildings. Fascinated, Skipper wandered around the set.

Soon it started to get dark outside. Skipper watched the lighting crew adjust the lights so that it continued to look just like daytime on the outdoor set. Suddenly she heard someone calling her name.

Skipper turned and saw Barbie's friend Ken. "Hi, Ken!" she called, walking over to him.

"Hi, there," Ken answered, leaning over to hug her.

Skipper put up her hands. "Hey, watch the makeup!" she scolded. "If you mess up this face, the makeup artist will kill me!"

Ken laughed and said, "Oh, that's right. You're an actor now. I forgot."

"What are you up to?" she asked him.

Ken explained, "I'm the **digital** effects **supervisor** on this movie. Along with the special-effects **technicians,** I'll be working on the scenes in which Diane's character is invisible. Later I'll be putting those scenes together on a special computer."

"Really?" Skipper replied. "That sounds pretty cool. I just love all that high-**tech** stuff. I've been learning about it in my computer class at school."

"Barbie mentioned that to me," Ken replied. "If you want, you can come and watch us work sometime. That is, if you're not too busy with your acting," he teased.

Skipper was about to answer when she felt a hard bump from behind.

"Oh, pardon me," a woman apologized.

"No problem," Skipper started to say. But when she turned around, she was standing face-to-face with Diane Burns. The movie star was no longer wearing glasses or a baseball cap. She was in costume. And Skipper noticed that Diane's makeup looked just as heavy as her own. "She's pretty," Skipper thought. "But she looks taller in the movies."

Diane stared at the teenager for a moment. Then she asked, "Did I bump into you this morning, too?"

Skipper nodded.

Diane looked embarrassed. "I'm very sorry.

I don't know why I'm such a **klutz** today. It must be my nerves. I'm always a little jumpy on the first day of shooting." Then she held out her hand and added, "I'm Diane, by the way."

For a moment, Skipper stood there, speechless. Here was a movie star who had made many movies, and still she was nervous. And this movie star wanted to shake Skipper's hand! "I'm Skipper," she sputtered.

Ken smiled. "I believe that Skipper has a scene with you, Diane," he told the older actor.

"Really?" Diane asked. "Maybe we could practice lines together before our scene. I promise I won't bump into you again."

Skipper laughed and quickly replied, "I'd like that very much."

Just then, Barbie came outside and made an announcement. It was time to quit for the day.

After Diane had left, Barbie walked over to Skipper and Ken. "I'm sorry you didn't get to do your scene today, Skip," Barbie said. "I hope you weren't too bored."

"That's all right," Skipper replied. "I had fun just learning about different people's jobs. I had no idea how many people it takes to make a movie!"

Skipper couldn't wait to get back to her dressing room and wash off the hot, heavy makeup. She looked at the time. It was already ten o'clock at night. She couldn't believe she had just spent an entire day on the set and hadn't done any acting!

Maybe her day had been long and a little boring, but at least she would have a chance to rehearse with a movie star tomorrow!

Chapter Four

The next morning started at 4:00 A.M. again. By the time Skipper arrived at work, some of the crew had already been there for hours, putting finishing touches on the set. The lighting and camera crews had also been there. They were trying to get the lighting just right for the first scene of the day.

"Good morning, Skipper!" Glenn called out.

Skipper waved back at the production assistant, trying to hide another big yawn. "I wonder when movie people get to sleep," she thought. She glanced over at the hotel set. Then she saw Diane sitting in a chair, reading her script.

"Diane likes to spend time on the set. It makes her feel more comfortable when the scene is actually filmed," Glenn whispered to Skipper.

"That makes sense," Skipper whispered back.

Just then, Diane looked up from her script. "Hi, Skipper!" she called out, walking over. "Would you like to rehearse our scene?"

"Oh, yes!" Skipper replied.

Skipper held her breath as she followed Diane. The movie star had a private trailer located near the set. It was so exciting, Skipper thought she might burst. Inside, there were several awards on the walls and pictures of Diane posing with other famous people.

Over in one corner of the trailer, Skipper noticed a clown suit. "That's strange," she thought. "I don't remember reading any clown scenes in the script."

At Diane's suggestion, they read through

the scene several times. The actress explained that she tried not to memorize her lines at all. "I read through the scene and try to understand it well enough so that the lines start to come naturally," she told Skipper.

After rehearsing the scene over and over, Skipper found her mind wandering. Diane was such a nice, regular person that Skipper felt brave enough to ask her a question.

"I was wondering," Skipper began, "do you ever get tired of all the rehearsals and waiting around?"

Diane shrugged and replied, "Sometimes I do. But, you see, I love to perform. It's part of who I am."

"But what about all those auditions, the early mornings . . ." Skipper broke off.

Diane continued, "The makeup that makes your skin break out, the endless rehearsals, the retakes? For me, it's all worth it. When I go out there, I become somebody else."

"Hmmm," Skipper thought. Then she smiled and said, "Just one more question?"

"Sure," Diane laughed.

"Why do you have a clown costume?" she asked, pointing to the corner of the trailer.

Diane laughed again. "I said I loved to perform, right? I also love children. Once a month, I go to a hospital where I'm not Diane Burns, movie star. I'm Dee-Dee the Clown. I perform for them, and, most of the time, I can make them smile. It's the best feeling. Your sister and Ken know about it, but they're the only ones. I try to keep it a secret. Some people are starstruck, you know. Not the kids, but other people. If they knew that I was a 'movie star,' then it would spoil it for everyone."

Skipper nodded. "I understand completely."

Then Diane added, "I'm going there tonight for a birthday party for Timmy, one of the kids."

Skipper was about to ask her another question when there was a knock at the door. It was Glenn. "Sorry to interrupt," he said. "But it's time to get into makeup and costume, Diane."

"Okay," Diane replied. Then she turned to Skipper and added, "Thanks for the run-through."

"Thank *you*. I'll see you later," Skipper called as she left Diane's trailer.

Skipper decided to watch the effects crew for a little while before heading over to get her makeup done. "The longer I can keep that stuff off my face, the better," she thought.

"We need some help over here!" a man shouted suddenly. "Skipper? Can you help us out?" It was Ken. He was helping the effects crew adjust the wind machine.

"Sure," Skipper answered.

"We need you to stand over there, under the street lamp,"

explained Ken.

Skipper hurried onto the set and took her place under the fake street lamp. Someone turned on the wind machine. A breeze started. Then the wind got stronger. Soon Skipper felt as if she were going to blow away! Then, suddenly, it stopped.

"Sorry," Ken said. "Was that too much?"

Skipper giggled. "Not if you want to make a **hurricane**!"

When her job was finished, Skipper decided to stay and watch. Then Diane came on the set, and the crew rehearsed the scene, using fake snowflakes to create a snowstorm.

After filming the scene once, Barbie asked them to do it again and again. Each time the cameras stopped rolling, the crew had to clean up the mess of "snowflakes" and start over again. Skipper wanted so much to ask somebody, "How did you make snowflakes that don't melt?"

Just then, Barbie announced, "That's it!

Thanks, everybody! Take a break for about thirty minutes. Then we'll start again and add everyone else."

Skipper sighed happily. "Finally," she thought. She hurried over to the makeup and wardrobe departments to get ready for her first scene.

During the scene, Diane's character would be arguing with the mean manager of a homeless shelter. He would tell Diane's character to stay away from the shelter. He would accuse her of spoiling all the children with toys and games.

Skipper and several other actors were called to the set. Barbie came out and spoke with them. "We want this to look like a busy city street," she said. Then she spoke to each person, explaining which direction to go in and how to act. "Skipper, I'd like you to walk past Diane right after she drops her package on the ground. Pretend you're speaking with someone else. You're upset that

Diane's package has gotten in your way."

Soon Barbie had finished with the actors. She then reviewed camera angles and discussed the lighting with the crew.

Finally it was time to film the scene. Skipper and the others took their places at the edge of the set. But Skipper was finding that she was more interested in what was going on *behind* the camera.

"Action!" Barbie called. The actors did as they were told. But when the scene was over, Barbie said, "Let's do it again." Then she asked Skipper and the others if they could keep their voices down. "You did a fine job," she explained, "but too much noise will take away from what the main characters are saying."

Then Barbie filmed the scene again. And

PROD
SCENE   TAKE
FEED/SHOOT
DIRECTOR
DATE

again! Skipper couldn't understand why they had to do the scene ten times!

It was getting dark by the time Barbie finally shouted, "That's a take!" She called the cast and crew together. "Good work, everyone!" she told them. "I know it's been a long day, but I have to ask some of you to stay late tonight. We still need to film one of the 'invisible' scenes. If we start right away, we should be out of here by nine o'clock."

Skipper happened to be standing next to Diane when Barbie made the announcement. The movie star let out a sigh. Skipper remembered what Diane had told her about the party for Timmy at the hospital.

Skipper turned and whispered to Diane, "What are you going to do?"

Diane shrugged. "I guess I'll just have to call the hospital and tell them they'll need to find somebody else. This happens quite a bit when I'm filming. I was just hoping to be there tonight for Timmy. He's only four years old."

Skipper felt sorry for Diane. "Is there anything I can do to help?" she offered.

"Thanks, but I don't think so," Diane replied. "Unless," she said, smiling, "you want to perform for Timmy in my place."

Skipper thought for a moment. Then she answered mysteriously, "I have another idea!"

"What's your idea?" Barbie asked. She and Ken were standing nearby. They had overheard everything.

"Is there any way someone else could stand in for Diane here?" Skipper wondered. "Then she could still perform at the hospital."

Barbie thought for a moment. Then she replied, "Well, we're shooting one of the invisible scenes. I guess Diane doesn't really have to be here. We just need—"

Ken broke in, "Someone about Diane's size.

Skipper could be Diane's body double! They're about the same size. She would just have to be able to perform her actions well."

Diane added, "That's a wonderful idea! I'm sure Skipper could do it. That is, if she doesn't mind." The three adults turned and looked at Skipper.

"Why not?" Skipper answered. Then she thought, "It would give me a chance to check out this special-effects stuff."

"Then it's decided," Barbie declared.

Skipper turned to Diane. "You had better get into your clown costume. You don't want to be late for the party, after all."

Diane smiled warmly. "Thanks, everyone," she said. Then she hurried off.

A little later the wardrobe mistress was helping Skipper get into Diane's "blue suit." It was just as Ken had explained it to her. A blue bodysuit covered Skipper from her neck to her toes. She would be almost completely blue. Over it, Skipper put on Diane's skirt, blouse, and shoes. Then the wardrobe mistress handed Skipper a blue stocking made of light nylon that was thin enough to see and breathe through. Before she went on set, Skipper would pull it over her head.

After the scene was filmed, Ken would use the computer to block out all the blue parts. In the final cut, it would look like the actor was invisible and the clothes were moving on their own.

"I think you're ready," the wardrobe mistress finally stated.

Skipper giggled. "I feel like a blue mummy."

"And you look like one, too!" the wardrobe mistress said with a laugh.

Skipper thanked her and walked out toward the set. There was no one in sight. The crew was still taking a break. Skipper walked around a corner and bumped right into somebody. "Oh, I'm sorry!" Skipper apologized.

"That's okay. I've done my share of bumping into you," the other person replied.

"Diane?" Skipper asked, laughing. Standing in front of her was a fully dressed clown. She had a big mop of orange hair, a white face with bright blue lips, a big red nose, and giant, floppy shoes.

The clown nodded.

"Wow," Skipper cried. "You look great!"

Diane laughed. "You, too!" she said. "No one will even know it's not me once you put that blue stocking over your head. Thanks for doing this, Skipper. It means a lot to me and to the birthday boy, too."

"You're welcome," Skipper replied. "I can't wait to see how this is done!"

"Have fun!" Diane called as she left.

A little while later, Skipper met with Barbie and Ken. Barbie explained the scene to Skipper.

"Do you remember the scene we filmed

MAKE - UP ←

earlier today?" Barbie asked.

"Remember it? I know that scene by heart!" Skipper replied. "We only filmed it about ten times!"

Smiling, Barbie said, "That's good. We're about to film the scene that comes next. Diane's character has realized that she will get into big trouble if she gets caught at the shelter again. Still, she wants to keep the kids happy. So she decides to use her power to become invisible. Then she secretly delivers little treats to the kids in their rooms.

"It's a fairly simple scene," Barbie told her. "But the lighting and camera work have to be precise so that Ken can make you invisible on the computer later."

Skipper found she was more interested in watching Ken work with the lighting and camera crews than in her part. She listened to him carefully.

When it came time to film the scene, Barbie only needed to shoot it a few times.

"You did well, Skipper," Barbie told her

when they were finished.

"Thanks," Skipper replied.

Skipper was thrilled. "Now the fun begins," she thought. "I wonder if Ken will let me watch him work on the computer."

Later, Skipper walked over to Ken. "When will you do your computer work on this scene?" she asked.

"I'm not sure yet," he answered. "Why?"

"Do you think maybe I could watch you when you do it?" she asked. "I'd really like to see how the computer effects are done."

"Of course," Ken agreed. "But I thought you were more interested in becoming an actor."

"Acting is cool and everything," Skipper explained. "But I'm beginning to think that special effects are even better." The teenager laughed when she realized what she had said. "Who would have thought that I would ever say that! Just wait until Barbie hears!"

Chapter Five

On Monday morning, Skipper and Barbie saw Diane in the parking lot.

"Thanks again for allowing Skipper to stand in for me on Friday night," Diane said to Barbie.

"No problem," Barbie replied.

Skipper added, "You know, I really had fun."

"That's great," Diane told Skipper. "I did, too. And I think Timmy had a really happy birthday. I guess it all worked out for everyone."

Barbie continued, "I hope you're both ready for your scene together. We're scheduled to shoot it this afternoon."

"We are," Diane agreed. "I'll go get ready."

Skipper looked at Barbie and admitted, "I'm getting nervous again."

"Don't. You'll do fine," Barbie reassured her. "But we had both better get going."

That afternoon, Skipper and Diane did their scene together. It took place on the bedroom set that Skipper had seen on her very first day.

"That's a take!" Barbie called after one take.

"You mean we don't have to film the scene ten more times?" Skipper teased.

Barbie smiled. "That's right! Sometimes, but not often, the first take is the best one."

Skipper laughed. "I can't believe that after all that work my scene is over already!"

"Welcome to the movie business," Barbie said. Then she added, "You have talent, Skipper. Do you still think you want to be an actor?"

Skipper paused. "Well, I like acting," she began, "but I don't love it the way Diane does.

She says she really doesn't mind all the rehearsals and the waiting around. She says it's worth it to her. I think I may be more cut out for special effects."

Barbie smiled. "You mean you're not cut out for champagne and caviar? But seriously, it's good to be **flexible.** The important thing is to keep trying things you like until you find what you like the most."

A couple of weeks later, Skipper got a phone call from Ken. "It's time to edit your scene," he told her. "Do you still want to come over and watch yourself become invisible on the computer?"

"You bet!" Skipper answered. Ken picked her up the next day and brought her to work at his studio. Skipper watched him for hours as he worked on each frame of the movie. He used a digital pen to draw on the screen. He even let Skipper do some of the editing, too.

It took hours, but, for Skipper, the time flew by.

Skipper didn't once feel bored. In fact, she had never been so fascinated with anything in her entire life!

Later that night, Ken drove Skipper home. They had dinner together with Barbie.

Skipper was so excited, she couldn't stop talking. "I helped Ken make me disappear right on the computer screen! He also created this really neat glow around me. It was amazing!"

Barbie smiled. "We call it 'movie magic'!"

"Well," Ken said, "I just got a job that starts soon. It's a horror film with lots of special effects. We'll be working with models and computer graphics. Would you like to work on it with me?"

"Do you mean it?" Skipper asked.

"Yes," Ken told her. "But you'll have to cut back when school starts in September."

"That's okay," Skipper said.

Barbie added, "Maybe you could talk to

your computer teacher about getting extra credit for your work."

"Good idea," Skipper agreed.

Ken explained, "I'll show you different makeup and lighting **techniques.** And how to make models and do other amazing things with computers. You know, we'll even be adding cartoon characters to the live-action movie."

"I can't wait!" Skipper cried.

"You're going to have a great teacher," Barbie told Skipper, "no matter what you do."

When dinner was over, Skipper cleared the table and brought the dishes into the kitchen. Then she returned to the dining room. "Hey," she blurted out, "I was wondering about something. If we used blue dishes, would we be able to make them invisible after dinner?"

Barbie laughed. "I'm afraid not, Skipper. We still haven't figured out how to get rid of dirty dishes—except by washing them!"